CUP OF LIFE

THE EVERLAST TRILOGY BOOK 3

JULIANA HAYGERT

COPYRIGHT

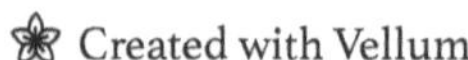 Created with Vellum

1

———

THIRTY OR FORTY YEARS AGO, I WOULDN'T HAVE STARED AT THE girl in front of me for more than five seconds before charming her into going to bed with me.

But this girl ... this girl was different.

"I think that's everything," Nadine said, stepping out of the cottage as Rok flew from the roof.

It was early January. The lights around the cottage reflected off the three feet of snow and illuminated Nadine's long brown hair, tinting some strands bronze. Her hair, her dark green eyes, and her red lips contrasted with her fair skin; the only thought on my mind was that I had never seen a more beautiful girl in my entire life. And I had been alive for quite some time.

Nadine approached me, and as it was every time she looked at me, I fought the urge to reach to her, to pull her against me, to kiss her, to—

"It is everything, isn't it?" She glanced at the bag slung across my shoulder and the box in my arms. She held her sister's stuffed bunny in one hand and a duffel bag in another.

We had been moving to our new location all day, making several trips to and from, and now we were the last ones here.

"I think so," I replied, quickly glancing to Rok hovering above our heads. "Ready?"

She walked down the porch steps, into the snow, and turned to the cottage. Her eyes scanned it, as if she wanted to take every little detail with her.

She slung the duffel bag over her shoulder and flipped the collar of her jacket up. "It's odd. I feel like I should feel bad for leaving this place after fleeing so many others, after losing so many people." She sighed. "But I don't, and I totally should, especially after seeing the new place Ceris got us."

I nodded, knowing too well that the new place brought her depressing memories.

No matter. It was a new place, a new path on our journey, a new beginning. We were on the right track.

I offered my arm to her. "Let's go, darling."

With a half-smile that made my heart skip a beat, Nadine sauntered to me and hooked her arm with mine.

I scooted closer to her, closer than necessary because I could and because I wanted to, and then I transported us out of there.

NEW FREAKING YORK FUCKING CITY. THAT WAS WHERE CERIS found a couple of intact buildings and apartments, one of the few Omi and the demons hadn't completely destroyed when they invaded the city over a month ago. She had found many bodies in them though. Levi, Izaera, and I helped her clean the large third floor, four bedroom apartment she had chosen before she brought the others to the city.

"They will never look for us here," Ceris said, using her powers to scrub the walls clean of blood.

She was probably right, but I knew Nadine wouldn't be okay with it.

When we brought the others, Nadine didn't disguise her disgust, but made no other objections. She understood why Ceris had chosen this place, and she agreed with the goddess's reasons. Still, it wasn't easy for her.

"Are you all right?" I asked as we walked among the debris, rumble, and flipped cars that lined the area around the apartment.

Ceris, Levi, Izaera, and I had united our powers to build a strong ward around the place with a radius of three blocks. Then we cleaned paths that led to the building while moving bodies, cars, and broken glass out of the way.

"I'm fine," she answered, pointing the flashlight to our improvised trail. She wrinkled her nose at the smell of the decay and avoided looking around too much.

We arrived at the building, crossed through the front doors, walked up three flights of stairs—the elevator was destroyed—and opened the door to the apartment.

It wasn't bad. A large living room with a fireplace, two sofas and four armchairs, a coffee table, lamps, and other decorative stuff, though most we had to throw away. Vases, pictures, paintings, rugs, pillows—all broken or tainted by blood—were now in the trash. Then there was a dining room for ten and a fully equipped kitchen. There was an office and half-bath in the front. Next to them was a corridor that led to four bedrooms, one being a suite, and two separate bathrooms.

We had to replace most beds, comforters, and pillows, since those had also been destroyed during the invasion. We had to find generators and fuel for the electricity, and we had gone to a grocery store in Australia—so not to leave a trace around here—for food and drinks.

We took all the furniture from the front office and transformed it into a gym. It was half the size of the gym we had in northern Greenland, but it was a place to burn some energy and stay sharp.

Ceris and Levi had chosen the suite. Apparently, they were mending things between them. Zelen and I were sharing one of the bedrooms, while Izaera shared another one with Keisha. Nadine had picked the spare room all for herself. Lucky girl.

I dropped the box in the living room as Nadine walked to the door of her bedroom and stared at the inside.

"What is it, darling?" I followed her gaze. The furniture we had found was simple. A brown wooden queen bed and matching nightstand, thin mattress, and a dark blue comforter. Nothing else. No curtains, no rugs, no decorations, no drawer, no dresser—the same as the other bedrooms.

"It's so lifeless," she muttered. "If the bed was made of metal, I would think we were in a prison."

A prison. That was what this was for her. This situation, this place, this war, the Soul Oath. Her prison.

I leaned closer to her and kissed the top of her head, not sure what to say. She turned to me, with suspicion in her pretty eyes, as if she doubted my intentions. I guess she had no reason not to suspect my intentions. She once said she was tired of my mixed signals. I was too, but I couldn't help myself. I tried with all my might to stay away from her, to not touch her, not hug her, not kiss her. So far, I was failing.

"Come on, darling. You love it when I kiss you." Teasing came naturally to me, and she actually reacted the way she always should react with me: her brows knotted and she dismissed me. I should have stopped there. I should have walked away and left her be. Instead I nudged her arm with my elbow. "What?"

"Nothing," she said, her tone indicating it wasn't really nothing. She sighed and stepped into her bedroom. "I guess I better ..." She gestured around the room, and I had no idea what she meant.

Nevertheless, I went along with it. "Sure. Yeah."

She closed the door in my face.

2

FIRST NIGHT IN THIS APARTMENT AND SLEEP DIDN'T COME easily. It was all Zelen's fault. Apparently, he had decided his snores should wake the entire block.

Tired of tossing and turning, I got up. Ceris had made sure the heat was on and set to a high temperature before going to bed, so I left the room in my pajamas pants and without a shirt.

Barefoot, I walked along the hardwood floor trying not to make a lot of noise. I halted when I entered the living room, not sure what I wanted to do. There was no TV, no radio, and no books. I could exercise a little—I guess burning some pent-up energy wouldn't be a bad idea—but I would probably make a lot of noise and wake everyone.

In the end, I headed to the kitchen, grabbed a beer from the fridge, and sat on one of the stools around the island. I took a long swallow of the cold drink. Bah, I hadn't drank any beer in so long. In little over three months actually, but it felt like years.

The chilly liquid went down my throat, and I let out a huge "ah" of satisfaction.

Damn, the thing was good.

On instinct, my left hand went to the necklace around my neck. I was able to control this gesture when around others and when focused on something else, but alone? I always ended up touching it. Which was ridiculous. It belonged to the human who had carried me for nine months, the one who raised me as her child. In some twisted sense, I had been her child, and she had been my mother.

For some reason since restoring my memory, I was weirdly unsettled about my feelings for the humans who had been my parents. Until then, I had loved them. I had adored them. I wanted to avenge them, remember them, keep their tokens. Then everything changed, but I still couldn't take off this damn necklace.

Nadine had been right, as usual—not that I would ever admit it out loud. To convince me to strike the Soul Oath with her, she tried to make me understand how much she needed to do something for her family by reminding me of my own. Back then, I would have done everything for them. *Everything*. That was why I ended up accepting the Soul Oath.

Granted, when we made the deal I was sure I could repress my feelings for her. I was sure she was nothing more than something pretty to look at. However, I was kidding myself because she had already reached deep into me, and I didn't want to admit it. Silly me because now the time was passing; it was flying, and I didn't know how to fix this fucking oath.

The problem was, I knew there was no fixing it. I didn't

want to accept that, so I tried not thinking about it. I tried to not remember I had screwed up.

I finished the beer and considered going back to bed but decided Zelen would keep snoring, and I could use another drink. I threw the empty bottle in the trash and opened the fridge.

I closed it when I heard mumbling.

I kept still, paying attention to it. The mumbling sounded louder this time, and I followed it. I ended up facing the first bedroom's door. Nadine's.

"No," I heard her voice through the door. "Oh, God, please, no!"

Knowing exactly what was going on, I swung the door open and entered the bedroom.

"Nicole," she whimpered, thrashing in her bed. "No, no!"

I closed the door behind me and rushed to her side. "Nadine," I called her, touching her shoulder. "Wake up, Nadine."

"Oh God, Morgan." Then she screamed.

I grabbed her upper arms and shook her, not too hard but not too gentle either. "Nadine!"

Her scream died out, and her eyes flew open.

"It was just a nightmare," I said. Her lips quavered before she hid her face behind her hands. "It's okay, darling, you're safe."

She shook her head. "But they aren't," she said, her voice breaking.

For a moment, I was undecided about what to do. Just pat her arm, tell her she was okay, and leave? That would be the right action. I had to keep my distance from her.

I groaned. Who was I kidding? I knew exactly what I

wanted to do, and for once I did it. I pulled back her comforter and slipped under it with her.

She peeked at me through her fingers, and I held back a chuckle.

I lay in her bed and opened my arms for her. "Come here." Her hands slipped away from her face, and she stared at me with teary eyes. "I'll take care of you. Come here."

She scooted closer, turning her back to my chest and fitting her tight little ass on my hips.

I took a hard inhale. By the Everlast.

What the hell? This was paradise, and I was going to enjoy it. I put my arms around her waist, placed my head on the crook of her neck, and inhaled deeply again, savoring her sweet wild rose scent and her perfect, warm body—clad in a skimpy tank top and shorts—pressed to mine.

She sniffed and I tried snapping out of it.

"Want to talk about it?"

"It was the same nightmare," she whispered. "But Morgan was there this time. He told me it was my fault, that I didn't give him time to change back."

"Darling." I placed a soft kiss on her shoulder, and she shivered shaking against me. I bit back a groan, desperate to jump on her, run my hands on her body, kiss her ... I sighed, concentrating on her current problem. "It wasn't your fault. If you want to blame someone, blame me. You were trying to save me, and I'll be forever thankful for that."

"I know. But it doesn't change the fact that I killed a human."

I brushed her hair away from her face and back to the pillow under us. My fingertips lingered on her neck. "You'll be all right, darling. Everything will be all right."

She took a deep breath, pulling my arm that was over her

tighter. My hand, guided by her, landed an inch under her breast. I wasn't complaining.

"I know," she said. "It's painful, but I'll make it. It won't be long now until the Soul Oath is complete and I'll have peace." I stiffened. Oblivious, she turned her head to me. "I will have peace, won't I?"

By the Everlast.

She would. I wouldn't.

As if I could protect her from the Soul Oath with my bare hands, I pressed her even tighter against me, resting my forehead on her cheek. "I—"

She squirmed, which didn't actually help my cause. "Ouch, you're gonna squeeze all the air from me."

Sighing, I loosened my arms, but only a little. "Sleep, darling. I'll take care of you now. I promise."

3

I LEFT NADINE'S WARM, SOFT BODY—AND HER BED—BEFORE she was awake. In fact, I got dressed and exited the apartment before anyone was awake.

I hurried to the border of the wards, careful not to slip on the new snow.

"Damn cold," I muttered, zipping up my leather jacket. I should have gotten something thicker and maybe some gloves and a hat too.

Fuck that. Where I was going should be warm.

Once outside the shield, I transported to a forest. The scent of moss and wet leaves invaded my nose even before I could process it was pitch black here. Wrinkling my nose because I hated those smells, I cast a flame of light over my palm and looked around. Tall, thick trees surrounded me, but they were still green, which meant I was in the right place.

I darted, weaving between trees, roots, and bushes. I slowed right before reaching the clearing. I stepped onto it, gawking at the cottage identical to the one on the Croatian island. I hadn't been here in decades, maybe a century.

Seeing light through the windows, I hurried to the door. It opened before I could knock. Hesitantly, I entered the tiny living space and found the Fates in front of the fireplace.

"Hello, Mitrus," they said in unison.

"We need to talk."

The three of them turned to me in a choreographed movement. They looked as if they were made of pure magic. Their faces lacked wrinkles, but they still appeared old and wise with their silver hair, gray eyes, and too pale skin. I had always thought of them as witches since I first heard the term thousands of years ago.

"We cannot help you," Lavni said, Witch Number Three of the Future.

"I know." I took a few steps forward. "But I need to try."

"You cannot alter the past," Mani said, sitting down on the ragged brown love seat. She was Witch Number One of the Past.

Changing the Soul Oath would be the best option, but also an impossible one. "I-I don't want to alter the past, I want to guarantee a future," I said, staring at Lavni.

She shook her head. "I'm afraid you wasted your trip, for we cannot help you."

Frustration laced my muscles, and I grunted. "Please, hear me out. Talk to me if you can, but if you can't, just hear me."

The three women exchanged deadpan glances; it got on my nerves. After a moment, they looked at me and nodded.

"We'll hear you," said Nay, Witch Number Two of the Present, sitting on a short stool in front of the fireplace. "But we can't promise to do more than that."

"It's okay." I stood at the edge of the living room, afraid if I got too close they would shut me down. I was a god all right, but the Fates were the ones who oversaw it all, who knew it all. They might not create the future, but they could change it if they wanted. If they saw fit. "I'll take what I can."

"Speak," Mani said.

I took a deep breath. "I've made a deal with a human. A Soul Oath. She offered her life, her soul, in exchange for her wish. I plan on bringing her back to life after it's done."

"You can't," Nay said. "The Soul Oath won't allow you to alter or break the deal, not even after it's done."

I started pacing. All right. I had thought as much, but I needed confirmation. I hoped I was wrong. Seeing as I wasn't, I told them about plan B. "The water of the Lake of Life heals deities, right? So it should do more for humans, like grant eternal life? If I give her the water of the Lake of Life, she should be able to cheat death."

"No," Lavni said. "That water is made for deities only. If a human drinks it, she'll die."

"Wait. But Levi drank it."

"For one, he drank a small amount, just enough to give him a little strength. Second, his body was human but not his soul."

There went my plan B along with any hope I had.

"There must be something I can do," I muttered. Keeping my cool in front of the witches was harder than I thought it would be.

"You shouldn't have accepted Nadine's deal," Mani said. "Now it's too late."

Determination was a beautiful thing. I halted and stared at them. "No. There must be something I can do." They looked at each other, and I knew I was getting somewhere. "Please. Nadine can't die. Not now, not ever."

"Why?" Lavni asked.

Why? The question caught me by surprise.

I thought of her. I thought of Nadine, how beautiful she was, how her touch wreaked havoc inside me, how her kisses set me on fire. However, there was more to her than just the physical stuff. She was loyal, just, kind, dedicated, strong, and completely selfless. To me, she was perfect.

"Because—"

"You love her," Nay said.

Did I? I hadn't loved anyone in so long. In fact, other than my human parents, I hadn't loved anyone ever. Did I love Nadine? Maybe. Probably.

"I just ... can't bear to think of living forever when she can't. My existence won't mean anything without her."

Mani narrowed her eyes at me. "And that's not love?"

"Perhaps," I said. Why was it so hard to admit what I was feeling?

"What if she doesn't want to live forever?" Lavni asked.

Oh. *Oh.* I hadn't actually thought of that. I mean, who wouldn't want to live forever? Nadine, attached to her family the way she was, wouldn't.

My shoulders sagged. Here I was, trying to find a solution for a problem that didn't exist. Damn it.

But ... but if I found a way of making her immortal, I could tell her about it. I could show it to her and ask her if she wanted it. Of course, I would try to sell immortality to her, even though I already told her it was lonely at times—but it wouldn't be lonely because we would be together. In the end, it would be her decision.

"I promise I won't force her," I said. Her rejection would hurt like the pit of fire in the underworld, but I would never force her into a life she didn't want.

"You shouldn't interfere with this," Lavni said.

"I don't care," I said, hearing too well the begging tone in my voice. "Please, tell me there is an alternative. Tell me Nadine doesn't have to die."

The Fates looked at each other again. Mani and Nay rose from their seats, and the three of them joined hands, closing their eyes. They were communicating, seeing the future, or whatever else they did before reaching a decision.

They opened their eyes and stared at me.

"There is a legend," Nay said. My heart raced at her simple words.

"Thousands of years ago," Mani started, "a human found the Lake of Life. She was about to drink from the water, expecting to find immortality, when a lesser god, one of the Lake of Life protectors, entered the cave and saw the woman. He told her the truth: she was a simple human, and because of that she would die after drinking the water meant for gods. However, the protector became instantly enchanted by the beautiful woman and promised her he would find a way to make her immortal. He took a golden cup and filled it with the water from the Lake of Life. He went on a difficult series of quests. In the end, he was able to the turn the water from the lake into an immortality elixir for humans."

A glimmer of hope bloomed in my chest. "Wait. What was this difficult quest? What did he do?"

"The details of his quests aren't to be known, for this action is not to be repeated," Lavni said, sounding exactly like an evil witch.

"But if I don't find out about his quests, how I am supposed to—?"

"The story isn't finished," Nay said. "Listen."

I shut my mouth, impatience and anger rolling in my stomach. I blinked, focusing on my hope instead.

"The protector brought the cup back to the woman. She

drank from it and became immortal. However, immortality didn't go well with her personality. She also wanted power. So it was her turn to go on a quest and strike a Soul Oath with Imha."

I gaped. "What?"

"The woman promised the protector's life in return for powers. Imha accepted. The woman fulfilled her part of the deal and received powers from Imha."

"But ... I don't understand."

"The woman didn't drink all of the elixir. It is said she still has the cup and the immortality elixir. She calls it the Cup of Life, and she offers it to whoever wants it."

The glimmer of hope became a bright light inside me. "So, it's simple. I only need to find her."

"Yes and no," Lavni said, ripping at my hope. "There's a price. The woman, Nasya, only gives a sip of her water to those who pass her test."

The balloon of hope in my chest deflated a life. "What kind of test?"

"She chooses the test after meeting with the one who wants the cup," Mani said. "She tailors it accordingly."

I inhaled and exhaled, trying to remain calm. "I must meet her. I must find out what kind of test she'll ask of me. But ..." I raked my hand through my hair. I grimaced, still not used to how long my hair was now. I dropped my arms and sighed. "I have to find her first."

"We know where she is," Nay said.

I froze. The ribbons of hope in me grew again. "Then tell me."

4

I WAS READY TO LEAVE THE FATES' COTTAGE AND GO DIRECTLY to Nasya.

However, I had a duty to my creed, so I transported back to New York to talk to Levi, Ceris, and Izaera. Besides, I already missed Nadine. I could use one of her smiles before leaving to face the mysterious test.

Fuck. She probably wouldn't smile at me since I sneaked out of her bed before she was awake. Or maybe she would smile, glad I had been gone.

She complained about my mixed feelings more than once, but she also sent me mixed signals. One minute she was allowing me to get close, and the next minute she was clipping my wings. I knew I shouldn't advance on her, but whenever I threw caution out the window and tried to get close to her, her mood was hard to read.

Before entering the apartment, I sensed Nadine and Keisha training in the improvised gym. Damn. I would never get past them unnoticed, and I needed to talk to the other gods first.

I sent a quick mental message to Levi. *"Arriving. Meet me in your room with Ceris and Izaera. No one else."*

"You aren't in trouble, are you?" he asked, invading my mind.

"Not yet."

"By the Everlast." Then he was gone.

Taking a deep breath, I stepped into the apartment. As I suspected, the gym's door was open. Nadine—in tight yoga pants and a cropped blue bra top that did nothing to hide her gorgeous curves—and Keisha sparred with wooden swords. I stopped for a second, admiring the view. Nadine was getting better at combat, her movements fluid and sure, her posture and footwork nearly perfect. Her hair, pulled up in a ponytail, swished around her back, a wave accompanying her elegant moves. She was a vision.

And I was wasting time.

Shaking my head, I silently closed the front door behind me and started walking to the corridor.

Zelen appeared from the kitchen. "Morning, Lord Mitrus."

Oh fuck.

Nadine's arm went slack, her eyes shifting from her opponent to me, and Keisha almost hit her on the chest with her sword.

"What the—?" Keisha followed Nadine's line of sight. Her eyes widened and she bowed. "Lord Mitrus."

I groaned on the inside. How I hated these formalities. "Morning," I said, nodding at them.

Nadine didn't say anything, but she didn't need to. I saw the hurt flashing in her gaze before she put on a steel mask. She held my stare, trying to prove to me she didn't care.

"Mitrus," Levi called me from the corridor. "We're waiting."

"Right," I said, averting my eyes. I followed him down the corridor and entered his bedroom.

Ceris sat on the edge of the mattress, and Izaera took the chair in front of the vanity.

"What is it?" Ceris asked, always to the point.

Well, how to start it? What the hell, I was wasting time. "A month ago or so, I made a deal with Nadine," I blurted out.

"A deal?" Levi asked, sitting beside Ceris.

I took a deep breath. "A Soul Oath."

"What?" Levi shouted.

"So that's the deal I heard you two talking about at the volcano."

Levi turned to her. "You knew about this?"

Izaera shook her head. "No. I heard Nadine and Mitrus talking about a deal. I never thought it could be a Soul Oath."

"What did you promise her?" Ceris asked. "And what did she promise you?" Her face was deadpan, but her tone betrayed. She was worried.

"After ... after her family died, Nadine didn't want to live anymore. She even asked me in a teasing manner if I could kill her. But she wasn't teasing. She needed a reason to live, and she found one. She would learn how to fight and help us defeated Imha because she wanted a better world. Her motivation? After we win the war, I'll bring her family back to life in this better world." I paused, finding it hard to continue. "And she offered me her soul in exchange for theirs."

Levi cursed, Izaera puffed, and Ceris looked at me with hard eyes. "You did what? No, you're not that stupid. You didn't accept it, right?"

"I told you I made a deal with her. Yes, I accepted, but I

thought I could find a way around it, you know, being the god of the dead and death and all." I sighed. "But it isn't that simple. I went to see the Fates this morning."

"By the Everlast, this keeps getting better and better," Levi muttered.

I told them everything the Fates told me. About how I couldn't undo what the Soul Oath had done, how the water of the Lake of Life wouldn't cure her, and about the legend of the Cup of Life.

"I'm going to Nasya's island," I said.

"Wait a minute," Levi said. "I don't think I heard you right. You're gonna risk your life for a human?"

I frowned at him. "I thought you were all about humans."

"I am, but you aren't. Weren't. What is it?"

A knowing smile adorned Ceris's face. "Oh, but Nadine isn't any human to you, is she?"

I closed my mouth and held her stare. "No, she isn't. Besides, I'm a god. I can't die."

"That's not true and you're proof of it," Izaera said.

"Yeah, but I came back to life."

"At what cost?" Izaera shifted her gaze to the dark world outside the window. "We don't have another thirty years to wait for you. Moreover, the Fates confirmed your soul was lucky for awakening inside a human body. Next time you might not be lucky, and your soul could be lost forever."

"She's right," Levi said. "You know that in order to have a well-balanced world, we need all of us. Together. Alive."

"I know, I know. But I can't let her die. I just ... can't."

"I'm not sure about this," Levi said, shaking his head.

Irritation swam where hope had been a couple of hours ago. "What is your problem? You're against it because you had a thing for her? Now that she kicked your ass and you went back to Ceris, you want her dead? Is that it?"

"Mitrus," Ceris called, a warning in her voice.

"You're taking things too far." Levi raised his hands, palms to me as if offering peace. Peace my ass. "I don't wish anything but the best for her, but it was her wish. She wants to die. You should respect that."

"If it was four, five months ago, if she still cared about you the same way she did then, would you respect her wish?"

He stared at me, but I could see the conflicted emotions in his eyes.

Izaera spoke up. "Let's say you go to Nasya. You pass her test, and receive the Cup of Life. What will you do? Just show up here, open Nadine's mouth, and make her drink it? You have to consider she might not want it."

The same thing the Fates said. What was this? A sign I shouldn't even try? Fuck that.

"I know," I said. "I'll bring her the Cup of Life and tell her what it is. I'll tell her she'll be able to live while her family is alive, and—"

"But after her family has died, of old age or sickness," Ceris said. "Do you think she'll still want to live then?"

"I don't know!" I shouted. Remembering the others could possibly hear us, I lowered my voice again. "I guess I'll talk to her about all the possibilities and hope she chooses to drink from the cup."

"Meaning, you're hoping she chooses you," Levi added.

I glared at him, ready to jump at his throat.

Ceris rose. "You've changed, Mitrus. These past few months you have changed a lot. I can't believe I'm saying this, but it is a good change. I attribute that change to two things: your human family and Nadine. If she can touch your heart like that, make you a better god, a more just and kind god, then you have my support. Go forth, bring the Cup of Life back, and convince her of joining us in eternal life."

We all stared at her. Along with my bugged eyes, my mouth hung open.

"Everyone is surprising me today," Levi said.

Ceris had her half-smile back. "After knowing Nadine for over a year, I can attest she's a good person. A great person. It saddens me she and I aren't friends anymore, and she only puts up with me for the war's sake. Hopefully, she'll accept the elixir from the Cup of Life, and I'll have more time to earn her forgiveness."

Holy fuck. I almost asked Ceris to repeat all that so I could record it and play it back to Nadine. If I was surprised, she would have a heart attack.

"It's not a question of who she is," Izaera said. "She seems like a great person, yes, but is she worth Mitrus risking his life?"

No hesitation here. "Yes."

"His mind is set, my sister," Ceris said, her eyes on me. "He's telling us out of courtesy, just so we know where he'll disappear to. He's going no matter what. We better support him now."

Wow. Way to leave me speechless, and here I thought Ceris could be as evil as Imha sometimes. Perhaps I was wrong.

Levi sighed. "When are you going?"

"Now?" I said. "As soon as I leave this room and say goodbye to Nadine."

Izaera stood and patted my shoulder. "I'm not against this adventure, but I'm not in favor of it either. Just make sure to come back in one piece."

I nodded.

Levi grabbed my hand and shook it. "If this is what you want, then I'll respect your choice. Good luck, my brother."

My brother.

I hadn't heard that in centuries.

With a small smile, I shook his hand back. I looked at the three of them, relieved they understood me and energized they supported my decision, even if they didn't agree with it.

As odd as it was, they were my family and their support did matter.

5

———————

I RUSHED OUT OF THE BEDROOM AND INTO THE LIVING ROOM. Zelen had pushed the coffee table to the side and was meditating as usual, as Keisha ran on the treadmill in the gym. I walked around Zelen and peeked inside the gym.

Keisha tripped and almost fell. "My Lord." She bowed her head in an awkward way so as not to trip again.

"You're alone here," I said. It wasn't really a question since the room wasn't that big and I could see every corner of it.

"Yes. Nadine left a few minutes ago."

I glanced back to the corridor. Nadine's bedroom door was open. If she had been there, I would have noticed when I walked past it.

"Do you know where she is?"

"She mumbled something about fresh air and stomped out of here," Keisha panted.

"Thank you."

I hurried out of the apartment and flew down the stairs. I opened the building's front door, stepped out, and bumped into her. It felt like nothing more than a simple nudge, but

Nadine slipped back in the snow. I grabbed her hand and kept her steady.

"Sorry," I said at the same time she said, "Thanks."

"My pleasure, darling."

She slowly pulled her hand from mine, but she didn't break my stare. And we didn't move either.

Her cheeks were flushed, her ponytail was half-undone, and small fluffs of snow covered her hair. By the Everlast, she was pretty. Beautiful. I could stare at her all day.

She shivered. She had a heavy jacket on, but apparently it didn't do much as she was shrunk under it.

I stepped aside. "Get out of this cold, darling." Pressing her lips into a thin line, she entered the building, shivering. "If you're still cold, I can warm you up." I wiggled my eyebrows at her, trying one of my old tricks. I figured remaining the same cocky guy would be welcome.

Not so much.

Shaking her head, Nadine started walking to the stairs. No, no, no. I wanted to talk to her before she left. Before I left. But what could I say to her?

"Keisha said you went out for fresh air."

She whirled around, her cheeks redder than before. "Yeah. Not a good idea, considering everything smells rotten outside."

I chuckled. She didn't. In fact, she had a wary look on her face. I wanted to erase that wariness.

"Do you have something to say to me?" She held her chin high and buried her hands in the pockets of her jacket. I opened my mouth to answer, but she was faster. "Keisha told you where I was, so I'm assuming you asked her, which means you wanted to talk about something." Her irritated tone wasn't good on her. "But it seems you didn't."

She turned to leave and I stood my ground. "Wake up on the wrong side of the bed, darling?"

Going up a few steps, she mumbled a response. Something about alone and cold.

I rushed to her side, skipping a couple of steps to get to her faster. "What? What is it?" She kept on climbing the stairs, her jaw tight. I stepped in her way. "Talk to me, damn it."

She stared at me, an annoyed knot between her delicate brows. "Talk to you? I thought there was no talking here. You know, you come to my bed, sleep beside me, kiss my shoulder, breath on my skin, but talk? No. No talk, because you were gone in the middle of the night."

"Is that what this is about? You're mad at me because you wanted me to stay?" I leaned over her with a sneer. "You missed me in your bed, darling?"

She punched my chest, with more force than necessary. "Your cockiness was cute awhile back, but now it's starting to irritate me."

I advanced, going for the same step she was on, but she retreated. "What do you want from me?"

"I-I don't know," she whispered, taking another step back.

I descended to her step and pushed her back into the railing, closing my hands around the wood beside her waist. She gulped. I loved the nervous glint in her green eyes. "Let's see if this helps you make a decision."

I lowered myself, keeping my lips half an inch from hers. She closed her eyes and shivered, leaning into me. Undone, I groaned and closed my mouth over hers. She didn't hesitate and opened her lips for me, welcoming me with a brush of her tongue. Fire burned in me and something like a growl came from my throat. My hands slid from the rail to her waist, and I found out she had on the jacket and the cropped bra, but nothing else. I opened her jacket and spread my hands on her waist, enjoying her warm, soft skin. I pressed my body against hers, and she gasped, holding on to me.

By the Everlast, I could kiss her, touch her, and taste her every second of the rest of my existence. There was no way in hell I would ever get tired of this. Of her.

Because of that, I had to break the kiss, take my hands off her body, and leave her. Such thoughts killed me.

She pulled my jacket up and slipped her hands under my shirt, grazing my skin with her longs nails. This time I groaned, pressing my hips against hers. I felt the smile of her lips against mine, and my heart did that silly, girly fluttering thing. By the Everlast, she was kissing me and smiling. I was losing it.

Without breaking the mind-blowing kiss, I held her tight against me, lifted her up to twist us around, and placed her on the steps. Carefully, I lowered her back and head, then myself over her. As soon as my body touched hers again, she wound a leg around mine. Something raw, something deep stirred in me. I wanted her, every inch of her, and right now, right here, I knew she wanted me too.

That was why I had to leave.

Using all the will and some of my actual power, I started pulling away, but Nadine hooked both her legs around me and yanked me back to her. She wiggled her hips, fitting mine perfectly against hers.

"By the Everlast," I whispered, breaking the kiss. I ran my tongue down her chin and bit her neck. She cried in my ear, driving me crazy. A vivid picture of her, naked under me, moaning and gasping, invaded my mind. There was nothing else I wanted more in life than to be with her, please her, make her moan, make her smile, love her.

Love her.

I pushed against the stair and stood up.

She stared at me with big eyes as I retreated down the steps until I was on the ground floor.

Red rushed to her cheeks and she sat up, pulling her coat tight against her.

"Nadine, I—"

She raised a hand. "Don't bother." Blinking her eyes furiously, she stood and turned her back to me.

"Nadine, I need to go now, but I'll be back."

"Sure," she said, her tone sarcastic.

"Darling, I'll be back."

She paused on a step and glanced over her shoulder, wiping a tear from her cheek. Fuck, I made her cry. She obviously thought I was ditching her. Again. If only she knew how much it killed me to leave her. If only she knew I was leaving her for her own good.

"Don't ever call me darling again," she said through gritted teeth.

Then she hurried up the stairs.

I stayed there, watching her until she disappeared into the third floor hallway.

If I succeeded or not, I wasn't in a rush to see exactly *how* I was going to fix the shit I had buried myself in.

6

THE ISLAND WASN'T ON A MAP, AT LEAST NOT ON ANY HUMAN'S map.

It was a tiny little thing in the middle of the South Atlantic Ocean. At least it wasn't as cold here.

I transported myself to it and ended up on a long wooden dock that reached deep into the sea. Torches lined the beach, shining upon the white sand and casting eerie shadows over the crashing waves.

Taking off my jacket, I walked down the dock, approaching the beach. My wariness was on high alert, ready for any booby traps. I could feel the power of the island. I knew the test was coming at any time.

I halted at the end of the dock and scanned the sand. No booby traps, no attacks, no sound, nothing.

Did the Fates send me to the wrong place? They wouldn't do that. If they did, oh, I wou—

"Lord Mitrus, welcome," a sensual voice said.

I turned to my left. A beautiful woman paraded on the

sand, coming to me. She had generous curves and a translucent dress to cover them. As she approached, showing me an inviting smile, the torches illuminated her face. She was gorgeous with long, red hair, hazel eyes, tanned skin, and plump pink lips. I could see why she had instantly enchanted the protector. The woman exuded sex, and she definitely looked like she was going to try to trick me.

Let her try.

"Nasya," I said, stepping on the sand.

She stopped in front of me, and I confess it took every ounce of my will to gaze at her eyes and her eyes only.

Her smile widened. She reached one hand to my shoulder and sauntered around me, her fingertips touching me at all times, her honey scent wrapping around me.

"I don't receive many visitors," she meowed. "And the few visitors I have are usually humans who mistakenly stumbled upon the legend of the Cup of Life, or lesser gods trying to achieve more." She halted before me again. "I never thought I would see one of the almighties at my humble place."

Almighties? That was what they called us?

I shook my head and concentrated. "Is it true you still have the elixir of immortality?"

"Yessss," she purred.

"What do I have to do to get it?"

"Why would you want it?"

How insolent. A lesser deity questioning me. "It's none of your business."

"Ouch." She recoiled, feigning to be hurt. "I like it."

I counted to seven before asking again. I would have gotten to ten if it weren't for my lack of patience. "Will you tell me how to get to the Cup of Life?"

"Lord Mitrus, I heard stories about your beauty, your confidence, your"—she ran a hand down my chest—"masculinity, and I must say I'm not disappointed. In fact, with the current guarded expression you carry and the taught muscles on your arms, I'm enthralled."

I wanted to reach to her throat and squeeze the crap out of her. "Nasya, I'm here for the Cup of Life and only that. Now, tell me where it is."

She tsked. "You're not fun." She retreated a short step. "It's here, on the island."

"Where ex—?"

"But you can't simply take it. There are spells around it, preventing anyone from getting too close, even almighty gods. You won't get within a mile of it if you don't pass my test."

I inhaled, bracing myself. "What would be my test?"

She leaned closer, blinking her eyes at me, grin widening. "Sleep with me."

The woman was delusional, clearly.

"What?" I asked, taking a step back.

"A second ouch." Nasya waved her hand as if she had burned her fingers somewhere. "Oh, Lord Mitrus, you make me sad. You're the only man who has held on this long without looking at my body and drooling, and now you seem appalled by my simple test. You should have seen the tests I offered to others." She stepped closer again, purposely brushing the side of her hip on my thigh. "You're getting it easy—and good, I promise. I'm not that ugly. You can't tell me you don't want it."

I closed my eyes and inhaled deeply. No, she was not ugly. In fact, she was the opposite of ugly. Her voice, her eyes, her posture, everything about her screamed sex. Yes, I wanted to have sex. Who didn't? I had gone a long time without any release, and I wanted it badly. But when I closed my eyes, the one I saw brushing her body against mine, touching me, squirming under me, and gasping in my ear was Nadine. Only Nadine.

I opened my eyes and stared at Nasya. "You're crazy if you think I'll accept it." It was a bold move, but I didn't have too many options here.

"A third ouch. My, oh, my, Lord Mitrus, I like you more and more by the second." She turned away and stopped again several feet from me, posing her body in a way that flattered her curves. She pouted her lips and batted her lashes. "Unfortunately, that's the way it is. Your test is to sleep with me. To *pleasure* me."

My jaw tightened. I couldn't do this. I would never forgive myself. Nadine would never forgive me. However, if I didn't sleep with Nasya, she wouldn't let me have the Cup of Life, and leaving without it wasn't an option.

"A question," I spoke up, and she perked. "I thought your tests would be challenges, physical or mental. Sex is pleasure. Why that?"

She blinked at me apparently pleased with my question. "One. I can't leave this island, and I don't get many visitors. After so many nights using only my hands, I'm bored. I want something new, something better, and you are definitely that." She licked her lips, her eyes scanning my body. "You're more than that." Then her smile turned evil, and I saw a little of Imha in her. "Second, it is a challenge, isn't it? I can sense it, you know. Your heart. It belongs to someone. A human, I think. That's why you are here. You love her so much, you decided to come here and face whatever test I imposed on you. And yet you're hesitating, proving that sleeping with me is indeed a challenge."

Fuck. She couldn't be more right.

I could easily say yes and be done with it in thirty minutes—or less, taking into account how long it had been since the last time I had some. So simple. Do it, turn my back on this woman, grab the Cup of Life, and leave. Go back to Nadine and offer her the elixir. She would never know.

But I would.

Still, if I said no, I would go back empty-handed. Nadine wouldn't live forever. In fact, she wouldn't live another month, depending on how eager Ceris was to defeat Imha. And I couldn't deal with it. No fucking way. Nadine couldn't die. Not now, not ever.

I wondered what Nadine would do in my place. Being kind and loyal, she would never accept this test. She wouldn't betray someone she loved like that. She would put her love above everything else, and then she would find another way. Because Nadine was fantastic, and she always found another way.

And if Nadine was here with me, if she knew how much I cared for her and her feelings for me were mutual, if she knew about this test, she would tell me she would rather die than have someone she loves betray her. She would smile at me and tell me we would try to find another way, and if we didn't, she would die in peace. But until then, we wouldn't rest until we found another way.

Could I find another way?

I had to have faith. In the Everlast energy. In Nadine. In me.

"It seems I have wasted my time coming here," I said, retreating. "Farewell."

With the weight on my shoulders increasing by a ton, I turned and stepped onto the dock. By the Everlast, what a way to have my hopes crushed. I had been so eager, so sure that I would walk out of here with the Cup of Life. Fuck. What was I supposed to do now? How could I go back to the apartment and face Nadine after the way we parted without some peace offering?

I stepped to the other side of the island's protective shield.

"Wait," Nasya said. I glanced over my shoulder as she sashayed down the dock toward me. "I've always appreciated a loyal man." Her smile was gone and a new, gloomy light shone in her eyes. "When my man went on his quest to transform the water from the Lake of Life into something I could drink, he went through many rough paths, many tests, and many challenges. One of them was to sleep with a deity. He didn't hesitate. He slept with her, and he told me because in his mind he was doing it for me, so I could live forever with him. But I despised cheaters. Still do. That's why I killed him when Imha told me that was her wish in exchange for my powers. I did it, and I'm ashamed to confess I enjoyed taking that cheater's life. However, Imha always has the advantage. She gave me powers, powers that bind me to the Cup of Life and to this island. In the end, I'm her prisoner."

It all made sense now. Why she demanded a test for the Cup of Life. Why she had asked me to sleep with her, even after she had sensed my feelings for someone else.

"The question was the test," I said, astonished.

"Not exactly," she said, an almost innocent smile on her lips. "The question was the first part of your test."

"What?" I asked because I hadn't heard it right. "Two tests?"

"One test, two parts. Besides, I can ask for as many tests I want."

I looked around still wary of booby traps. "Is this some kind of trick?"

She offered me an innocent smile. "Lord Mitrus, I would never trick an almighty god."

I raised my eyebrows at her, suspicion spreading through my senses. "What's the next part?"

"I need proof of your intentions. I need proof that you, the god of death and the dead and the underworld, are indeed a good god, not an evil one. I need proof you really have changed this much and now love a human. I need proof you would do anything for her, that because of her, you'll be the most kind and just god there is."

I gaped at her. First, how the hell would I prove that? Second, kind and just? I thought she knew who I was.

I crossed my arms. "I just said no to you, doesn't that prove my feelings?"

"Forgive me, my Lord, but when it's so easy to lie, words don't mean anything. I need to see it, to feel it."

"And how are you going to do that?"

"It would take a little trip inside your head."

"What?"

"I need to see your thoughts, search your memories, feel what you felt."

I ground my teeth. "And you have the power to do that?"

"I have the power to do whatever my tests require of me," she explained in a proud tone. "So, Lord Mitrus, will you let me perform the second part of your test, or not?"

I didn't want this woman probing my brain, looking into

memories and moments I wasn't proud of. Once she saw my past and how *evil* I was, I would fail the test. I knew it. However, that gave me a chance. Maybe she had an evil bone in her—after all, she did kill her lover for power—and searching my past maybe she would sympathize with me. If I denied her access to my mind, it was a certain fail.

Sighing, I uncrossed my arms. "Yes."

7

———

Nasya spun around, as graceful as a dancer, and guided me back to the sand. From there we took a wooded path that opened to a grassy patch.

Uncomfortable silence stretched as we walked down the path until it ended at a round stone slab over the grass. A stone armchair with a high back sat in the center, looking ancient and rough, with symbols carved on its base.

She gestured to the armchair. "Please, my Lord."

No backing out now. Holding my breath, I sat on the chair. I braced myself for something—a prickling, a jolt, an energy rush—but nothing happened.

I glanced at Nasya. "What now?"

She strutted until she was standing behind the chair. "Now, you relax."

Easy to say. Relax on a strange island with a woman that had a Soul Oath with Imha, while seated on a prickly chair.

I turned my thoughts to Nadine. This was for her. I could do it for her. I leaned against the back of the chair, rested my arms on the armrests, and closed my eyes.

Nasya's cool fingertips touched my forehead.

At first nothing happened. Then I felt it. Her power rushing from her fingertips into me, into my mind, prickling and hurting. I gritted my teeth and clutched the arms of the chair as the prickling traveled further into my head. The pain spread, squeezing my mind. I bit my lower lip, and it was all I could do not to scream.

The pain shifted and dizziness took over my senses.

I swayed with it and fell on my knees. I blinked, fighting against the darkness. When my vision focused, I looked around. It couldn't be ...

"What's this place?" Nasya asked, appearing by my side.

I stood up. "It's my chambers at the Crystal Castle."

My crystal bed sat right in the center of the room. Black covers adorned the bed, and black curtains hung from the canopy. On the right a large floor-to-ceiling window led to a crystal balcony, overlooking the bright blue ocean.

By the Everlast, I had forgotten how beautiful this place was.

Startling me, the double door opened and a man paraded inside the room.

"Is that ...?" Nasya trailed off.

"Me," I answered, gaping at my older self. The old me still had my build, my height, my eyes, but his hair was a bit longer, and stubble shadowed his jawline and chin.

Imha followed and threw herself on Mitrus's back, cackling like a mad woman. "Where do you think you're going?" she asked, reaching to kiss his neck.

He waved her off, disentangling himself from her. "Not now, Imha. I'm not in the mood."

She put her hands on her hips. "You're always in the mood."

He flopped on the bed, crossing his arms above his head. "Just leave me alone."

Of course, she didn't. Imha crawled on the bed, running a finger up Mitrus's chest. "We need to talk business, dear."

"Later," he snarled.

She ignored him again. "Levi and Ceris are impossible. All they want is to wait. Wait for the humans to do what? Destroy themselves while believing in anything but us? That's so unjust. I want to be there and help them destroy themselves."

"I want the same as you," Mitrus said. "I want the humans to know about us, to worship us, to die for us. But we won't change Levi's mind easily."

"Then we make him change." Her finger stopped moving on the button of his jacket. "We change him."

Mitrus tilted his head to her. "What?"

But Imha didn't answer. "Hmm, this would feel better if you were shirtless."

"Imha ..."

She snapped her fingers, for effect of course, and Mitrus's shirt and jacket were gone. "Now, this is better." She straddled him, running her nails around his muscles. "Why are you fighting this, dear? You like it." She dipped into him and licked his nipple.

Groaning, he clasped her wrists before sitting up. "You're impossible."

She leaned to him, hovering her lips an inch from his, and whispered, "The way you like it."

He kissed her, and then flipped her on the bed, trapping her under him.

Disgust and nausea swirled in my stomach, and I shifted

my weight, knowing exactly where this was going. By the Everlast, I didn't want to see this.

"So ... you and Imha, huh?" Nasya said. "I heard rumors of her and Omi."

"She also had affairs with Omi," I said through gritted teeth. "Can you control this freaking thing?"

Without answering, Nasya took my hand and everything around us became a blur for two seconds, before settling in another place.

We stood to the side of the throne room at the Crystal Castle. Omi was seated on his throne with Imha on his lap; they were kissing as if there was no tomorrow.

"I'm sorry," Nasya said.

I shook my head. Ugh, good riddance.

Yeah, that was my thought now, but I remembered what I thought then. I glanced to the doorway leading to the private chambers. As Mitrus walked out of the corridor, his gaze found the lovebirds going at it on a throne and he halted. His expression changed from shock to anger, and I could still remember his feelings. Jealousy. Pure jealousy, but not because he loved Imha. He didn't. He never did. But because he wanted to be the best and the first; he wanted to be everyone's choice for anything. And right now, Imha was with Omi. She had *chosen* Omi, and that hurt Mitrus.

He marched back into the corridor, and Nasya took my hand again, changing the picture.

We were still in the Crystal Castle, but it was dark out and soft light emanated from the crystals, creating a comforting place. Levi sat on his throne, and Mitrus paced around the fountain.

"You never listen to me!"

Levi sighed. "I do listen to you, but you forget we are a team. I don't decide anything, not alone, and neither do you."

"Then we must talk to the others, decide on something," Mitrus said. "How many times am I going to have to tell you before you do something? Before you urge the others to do something? The humans are losing their faith. They don't believe in us anymore; most don't even know of our existence."

"I'm well aware of that."

"Are you? I don't think you are. Because if you were, you would be doing something about it. Without the human's belief, our powers will lessen and their precious world will suffer for it. Is that what you want?"

Levi rose to his feet. "Of course not! But we can't just parade through their cities, expecting them to wrap their heads around the fact that an entire creed of gods and goddess actually exist. Like you said, most of them don't even know of our existence. That action would cause too much damage, and we can't afford that."

Mitrus halted. "What do you suggest, then?"

"I don't know, brother. I don't know."

"You're losing your touch, Levi. You're growing weak. Keep this up and soon we'll be lost forever."

Mitrus marched out of the throne room, and Levi sunk back on his throne. From another door, Ceris strolled into the room and sat beside Levi, taking his hand in hers.

"We'll fix this, my love."

"I know. I just wish Mitrus could see that. I wish he would stop arguing with me and actually help me find a less drastic solution."

"Maybe you should talk to him again."

Levi scoffed. "Because that worked well the last three hundred times."

She leaned forward and kissed his temple. "He's your brother, love. He's your best friend, when he's not acting all righteous."

"Which is ninety percent of the time."

Ceris chuckled. "Well, that other ten percent, he's pretty good at being there for you, isn't he?"

Before I could hear his answer, Nasya grasped my arm and took us somewhere else.

I froze.

I knew Nasya would want to see everything about me, including my years as a human. I thought I had been prepared for it, but by the way my heart was pounding, I knew I wasn't.

We were on the back patio of the townhouse where I lived with my human parents in Israel. Little Micah kicked a soccer ball to the high wall surrounding the patio, pretending it was the goal.

"Score!" he yelled, raising his arms to the air. He couldn't have been older than nine.

My mother walked out onto the patio, and my heart paused. My knees wobbled, and I leaned against one of the high walls.

By the Everlast, how I missed her.

Wearing a long beige dress and a red hijab lowered on her shoulders, she walked to one of the gas lamps hanging from the walls to check it. She hated the darkness in the world and was afraid of the lamps running out of fuel and leaving us— them—in the dark.

"Did you see that, Mom? I scored!"

She smiled a true, wide smile, and my heart squeezed. "I

did. It was wonderful."

"I want to be a soccer player!"

She laughed and approached him, running a hand over the child's hair. "I know. You say that every day."

"How old do I have to be to join the country's team?"

"Older," my father said, appearing from inside the house. Like my mother, he was smiling at me.

Oh, by the Everlast, this was too much. My heart and my soul couldn't take it. I underestimated the effect these images would have on me.

From the corner of her eyes, Nasya watched me, her expression deadpan.

"I'll be older tomorrow!"

"Indeed," my mother said, leaning down to kiss the top of my head.

My father stopped by her side and put his arm around her shoulders. She leaned into him, and he kissed her cheek.

Meanwhile, little Micah's attention was back on his soccer ball, and he prepared to kick it again.

My mother turned around, scanning the patio for something, and then I saw it. The necklace around her neck. At home, she wore it over her clothes. When out, she tucked it in. I lifted my hand and pulled the necklace from under my shirt, squeezing it in my palm.

"Does it mean something?" Nasya asked.

My first thought was not to answer her, but she was here judging my past and perhaps any information would help.

"My father gave it to my mother when I was born."

She leaned closer to look at it. "Odd shape."

"Not once you see what it actually is. A twisted, closing heart with a smaller heart inside it." I pointed toward the sides of the bigger heart, closing over the smaller one. "My father said the bigger heart was for their love, and the smaller heart was me. I was surrounded by their love."

The back of my eyes burned.

Fuck.

I focused on the child, who was cheering a new goal, while my mother and my father clapped at him, encouraging him to do it again. Pride shone in their eyes and their smiles. I felt their pride rushing into me, warming my core.

Without warning, Nasya closed her hand on mine and took us out of there. I opened my mouth to protest, but closed it when I looked around.

Eighteen-year-old Micah was crouched along a wall in a dark alley, a hoodie over his head, shaking like bamboo in the wind.

Pain coursed through my chest. I remembered this moment. It was right after my parents were killed. Right after I killed the men who had killed them. I couldn't go home, not yet because I would expect to see my parents there and I would break down once I realized they were never coming back.

Micah looked at his hands with disgust. A groan escaped from his throat, and he knelt, bending his torso forward and punching the ground.

The flap of wings echoed through the alley and he shot up, scanning the area.

Rok came into view, slowly approaching Micah, who seemed wary of the bird.

"Shoo," he said, waving the raven off.

However, Rok was stubborn and kept advancing until he landed on Micah's shoulder.

"A raven on my shoulder." He snickered. "That's random." Rok, though seemed completely at ease. Micah stared at the bird, and I remembered this part as if it were yesterday. Rok's name popped in my head, as if I could remember him. "Rok. Hello, I'm Micah."

Rok cawed, and Micah smiled.

The bird cawed again. And again. And again—the sound becoming more urgent. Then the raven flew up and around him.

"What is it?" he asked, watching as the bird revolved above his head.

"Stupid," I muttered, watching the entrance of the alley, knowing what came next.

Screams sounded outside the alley, becoming louder with each passing second. Then a girl entered the alley, running and screaming.

"Help!" she yelled.

Micah watched her, paralyzed.

"Help!" she yelled again, running to him.

He looked up, sensing an aura for the first time, not knowing what it was, not understanding what the fuck he was feeling. I looked up too. There wasn't anything to be seen there, not with how dark the sky was.

The girl kept coming at him, but before she could get too close, a shriek resonated through the air and a giant bat fell over the girl, pinning her to the ground with its sharp talons. It opened its wings wide and bared its teeth into a snarl.

The girl screamed.

I took two steps toward the demon, before remembering I couldn't do a damn thing here. I turned and saw Micah still frozen in place.

"Wake up, stupid," I said to myself, as if I could change the past.

The bat lowered its mouth toward the girl's face, and

finally Micah moved. He grabbed a piece of broken wood from the ground and advanced toward the demon, shaking and nervous.

"Get off her!" he said, sounding more confident than he felt—I knew that.

But it was too late. The bat had already sunk its teeth into her shoulder, and its claw tore at her stomach.

Micah took two more careful steps, and the demon stopped ravaging the girl's body, lifted its head, and stared at him. The demon tilted its head as if it also didn't understand what it was feeling.

"Get off!" Micah yelled, advancing. "Go away!"

The demon did retreat. I remembered thinking it was because it was afraid of what I could do with my wooden stick. It was only after a few more encounters with them that I realized the demons were actually retreating because of me, though I had no idea why.

Micah swung the wooden stick toward the demon, and it flew away. He looked at the mangled body at his feet and dropped the stick. He fell on his knees and caressed the face of that strange girl.

I crouched beside him, knowing that guilt was eating him alive. Guilt for not having acted faster and saved this girl, and guilt for not having saved his parents. The same guilt that still swam inside of me.

Nasya touched my shoulder, and the world around us changed.

I glanced around, recognizing this place. NYC before the attack that destroyed the city. Nasya and I stood on the sidewalk, one block from NYU's south gate, two buildings from Nadine's old apartment.

"What are we looking for?" Nasya asked, also looking around.

I pointed to our right.

Nadine strolled out of the south gate. She clutched her tote tight and looked over her shoulders every few seconds. It was sheer dumb luck that she didn't see a younger Micah following her.

This had been the first time I saw her, a couple of days before saving her from the demon attack.

When I discovered I could sense auras and repel bats, I sold my parents' place, put all the money into a bank account, and used it to travel around, searching for auras like mine. I had been in numerous places, but no aura was out of the ordinary, until I stopped in New York and sensed Nadine. I had barely booked a hotel room and bought my Harley Davidson—because I intended to travel the United States with it—when I felt her.

Nadine stopped at the magazine stand beside me and picked up a newspaper. I glanced at it—the cover said something about a volcano, but who cared about that when I could stare at her without looking like a creep?

"That's the human you want to save," Nasya said. I didn't have to answer because Nasya knew. "She's beautiful."

Oh, I knew that. Everyone knew that.

This was the moment. The moment everything changed. One, because I had found someone with an aura that resembled mine. Two, because I met the girl who would change me forever.

Nasya took my hand. "Come on," she said, before changing the picture around us.

I wanted to complain about it because I wanted to look at

Nadine some more, but when I saw where she had taken us, I was actually glad.

Micah stood in the middle of a hotel room, wearing only jeans, and Nadine emerged from the bathroom. She stared at him, at his shirtless chest, and her cheeks grew pink. I smiled. Her reaction to me always made me smile.

"Hi, darling," Micah said.

She stopped in front to the mirror to comb her hair. "It's not that warm in here."

"I know." Micah laughed. "I need your touch and thought being shirtless would make the deal more attractive. Plus, you would want me more."

She turned to Micah, her mouth open. "Want you more? Are you insane?"

"No." Micah sat at the edge of the bed near her, his hand shaking. "Could you come here and help me?"

She walked to him and extended her hand. He grabbed her hand and, smiling, he pulled her closer, resting her palm on his chest. As she healed him, Micah closed his eyes and threw his head back, moaning.

Micah opened his eyes and stared at her.

"Are you better?" she asked, her voice quavering.

Nodding, he clasped his free hand around her other wrist and pulled her closer until she was standing between his legs. Still staring at her, Micah rose to his feet, brushing his body to hers. Nadine seemed tense. He leaned into her, but she pulled back a bit.

He put a hand around her neck. "You want this," he whispered.

"No," she said, putting her hands on his chest to push him away.

Micah pulled her to him again, leaning down. His lips brushed hers, but a knock on the door made her jump back.

"Take me out of here," I said to Nasya through gritted teeth. I had forgotten that damn Levi came in and interrupted my good time.

With a party-pooper expression, Nasya grabbed my hand and took us to another place.

We were at Cathedral Rock with Nadine, Levi, Ceris, and me.

Screeches and ruffling of wings sounded overhead.

"By the Everlast, they're already here." Ceris turned to Nadine. "Goodbye, Nadine. I hope the Fates don't treat you well." She waved her hand toward Levi, and a pink wind enveloped him and her. Then they were gone.

The demons landed around the ledge of Grandmother Rock. Micah helped Nadine stand and stayed beside her.

"What's happening?" Nasya asked.

"We just found out what we are, and Ceris left with Levi," I told her, not really in the mood to explain everything.

The demons formed a circle around them, shrieking and growling. Micah held her arm and kept her close.

The creatures moved aside, and Brock stepped into the circle.

"Hello Micah. Hello Nadine."

Nadine gaped. "You!"

"Yes, me. Am I late? I thought all of your friends would be here too. Where is the third one? All right, let's change the question. What are you three?"

Micah snorted. "Power Rangers, ever heard of them?"

Nasya shot me an are-you-crazy look and I shrugged, proud of my sarcastic side.

"Amusing." Brock paced before them. "You see, if you

don't answer to me, I'll have no option than to take both of you to Lord Omi." He turned to Nadine, and she shivered. "Will you be a good girl and answer my questions?"

"Never," she snapped, sounding braver than she was.

Brock shook his head and stepped closer to her.

Micah put himself in front of her and snarled, "Leave her alone."

Once more, Nasya glanced at me, something like surprise in her eyes.

"I'm afraid we're going for a ride." Brock snapped his fingers and the demons advanced.

Micah fought the demons off as best as he could, but there were too many. Soon, he was overpowered, and Nadine was pulled away from him.

"No!" he cried.

I didn't even feel Nasya's hand on mine until everything around us shimmered and changed.

The other me paced around the conference room in the shelter in northern Greenland, while Ceris and Levi sat around the table.

"Two days," Micah said. "Two fucking days since Omi took Nadine. Do you have any idea what they could be doing to her? Oh, by the Everlast. I don't care. I'm going."

The other me marched to the door, but Levi stood and spoke. "Calm down, Mitrus. They probably want information, and to get it out of her, she must be alive."

Micah glared at him. "You mean they must be torturing her."

Levi averted his eyes.

Ceris stood then. "You can't march in there, Mitrus. That would be suicide."

"Do I look like I care?"

The same frustration and powerlessness I felt that day rushed through me, and I leaned against the wall, hating to relive these days.

Nasya glanced at me.

"I care," Levi said. "We can't lose you. The creed can't afford to lose you. We'll find a way."

"I have an idea," Ceris said.

Nasya extended her hand to me, and I took it. The picture shifted. We stood in the shelter's gym, watching as Nadine and other me made out on the floor.

Lust rippled through my body along with an urge to punch the guy that was touching her right now, even though I knew this was a memory and I was the guy. Oh fuck, I had touched her, I had felt her, I had kissed her, and she had kissed me back; she had touched me back.

Micah thrust into her, and she moaned. By the Everlast, I would lose it right here.

Then when she reached down to his waistband, he pulled away.

"What was that?" Nasya asked. "I thought you loved her."

"I was trying to stay away from her," I confessed. "She deserves much better than me."

She really did. I was a messed up man with a bad past, and I would never be able to make up for everything. She deserved to be with a man who was as perfect as she was.

With a smile, Nasya touched my arm. The gym disappeared, giving away to the cottage on the Croatian island.

The other Micah burst through the door, carrying Nadine in his arms. This was right after the battle in the volcano. Morgan had stabbed Nadine, and she was still bleeding.

Levi gestured to her bedroom. "Lay her on the bed." Micah did as instructed. "Now, give me space."

He scooted back but didn't leave the room. "No, I want to help. I want to—"

"Mitrus." Levi put his hands over Micah's shoulders. "You need to calm down, and I need space to work on her."

Keisha appeared at the door. "Come on, my Lord," she said, grabbing his arm.

"Levi …"

"I know," he said. "Don't worry. She'll be fine."

Nasya stepped closer to me and clasped my hand.

"Last stop," she said as the image changed. We were in the living room of the Croatian island cottage, and Nadine was on the porch, buried under a blanket and hugging Pinky.

The other me spied her through the window, thinking about her birthday gift. She had been so happy about it, and I had been happy to be able to do something nice for her.

"Lord Mitrus, you surprise me with each memory," Nasya said, smiling.

"What do you mean?"

"While I'm in your head, I'm not only seeing your memories. I can see what you're thinking too. In the present. While we went through all those memories, I saw them and felt them. I felt whatever you were feeling at that moment, and I was feeling what you were feeling now, while watching it again."

"Wait. What? Then why were you asking me questions?"

With a knowing smile, she extended her hand to me. "Come on."

Hesitantly, I took her hand.

8

____

M y head spun and the darkness along the edges of my vision slowly retreated.

"Lord Mitrus," Nasya called.

The spinning was gone, and my sight sharpened. I straightened my back, sure I would have an eternal back problem after sitting in this chair.

Nasya stood in front of me, her hands clasped together.

"So?"

"During the first part of the test, I wasn't sure if I believed your words. That's why I asked the second part."

I already knew that. "Okay."

"I felt everything the past you and the present you felt, and I must say I'm impressed. That first vision with Imha, the old you let her seduce him fast and you even enjoyed the game, but the present you was disgusted. When arguing with Levi, the old you wanted to create a problem. The present you wanted to slap the old you. When with your human parents, the longing and the happiness you shared with your parents overwhelmed me. After their deaths, you were sad, both in the old you and the present you, and I also felt how terrible you felt for not having helped that girl sooner. When you first saw Nadine, the past you was curious, even about how hot you thought she was, but the present you emanated love. I know how desperate you were to save her from those demons at the top of that mountain. I know how you wanted to protect her from yourself, which honestly, the past you would have never done. I know how you wanted to protect her from anything and everything. And that's why you're here." She took a deep breath and smiled. "You have changed, Lord Mitrus. You have become a good god. A kind and just god. The human had a large hand in it, and for that, I'll give you the Cup of Life."

My heart squeezed. "What?"

"You passed my test. The first one in over six centuries. Congratulations, Lord Mitrus." Nasya bowed, a more exaggerated and elegant move than Keisha usually did.

Relief washed over me. Thank the Everlast energy!

Eagerly, I looked around us. The stone slab, the armchair, and grass. "Where is it?"

She beckoned me to stand. "Come with me."

Without hesitation, I followed her down another wooden path, deeper into the island until it became a bridge. The water flowing under the bridge glowed an unnatural blue light, and it formed a ring around a small rocky island. There was a stone pedestal at the center of that island and a golden chalice on top of it.

Nasya halted before we reached the bridge and gestured to the island. "The Cup of Life."

That was it? I just had to walk to it and take it? It seemed too simple.

Wary but still eager, I crossed the bridge. Nasya stayed behind on the path.

I reached the edge and inhaled deeply before taking the first step onto the island. I moved forward but nothing happened. I guess I still expected booby traps or tricks.

My gaze shifted to the golden cup, and I forgot all about that. It was beautiful and big, the size of my forearm, and shiny, with several of the creed's symbols carved on the rim. It was powerful—very powerful. I reached for it, spying the translucent liquid within it. So this was the elixir of immortality. I closed my hands around it. Energy slipped into me and I welcomed it, rejoicing in the fact that I had gotten the Cup of Life. Nadine would be able to live forever ... if she wanted.

With a winning smile, I turned back to the bridge. I took the last step on the little island and was about to cross the bridge when I slammed into a wall. What the fuck? I clambered back, almost dropping the Cup of Life, and stared ahead. There was nothing there. Nothing visible. The power of another shield hummed around the island.

"How do I get past this ward?" I asked.

"You don't," a male voice said.

I turned to my left and gaped, ice flowing in my veins, but I made sure to wipe the surprised expression from my face quickly enough.

Amiel, Jed, Riel, and Keon stood beside Nasya. Smiling the same easy grin that was my trademark, Riel put his hand around Nasya's throat.

"Do as we say, and she lives," Jed threatened.

I locked the new Mitrus away and put on my old mask. "And why do you think I care?"

"You're different now," Keon said. "You associate with

humans. You care for them, which means you care about any living creature, immortal or not."

I scoffed. "As if I care. She's a traitor." I glared at Nasya. "You talked about your hate for cheaters and traitors with pride, and yet you're one. You tricked me so they could sneak up on me."

"No!" she croaked. "I didn't. I swear, I didn't know they we—"

"Quiet!" Riel shouted, tightening his grip around her neck. She whimpered.

"We've tricked the both of you," Amiel explained. "We came here two weeks ago. We couldn't get to the cup. *She* couldn't get to the cup. The only way was passing her tests, which we didn't. So we kept an eye on the island, waiting for a fool to pass the test and take the cup."

"Imagine our surprise when you were the fool." Jed gestured to my hand. "Now we'll take the cup."

"Give us the Cup of Life," Keon commanded. "Give us the cup and we won't kill her."

I snorted. "She's immortal. You can't kill her."

"Is that right?" Riel pulled a Black Thorn from his back pocket.

My mouth felt dry. "How ...?"

"We stole it from Imha," Amiel said, sounding proud. "During one of her invasions. She was too busy fighting nymphs, and we were able to snatch it. With over a dozen of them, she surely didn't even notice."

They had me trapped and they had a Black Thorn. Fuck, this wasn't looking good.

I scanned the surroundings. There wasn't much to the island. The bridge, the wooden path, the large grass area, then the rocks and beach. I just had to cast a big bolt with enough energy to stun them, find a way of breaking the shield, run to the dock, and disappear.

Easy enough, if it weren't for the fact that I didn't know what or who was holding this shield up.

"Mitrus silent?" Jed teased, making a doubtful face. "That's new."

"See? He *is* different," Keon said.

I ignored their comments and asked a burning question. "What do you want the Cup of Life for?"

"It's actually a funny story," Amiel said, grinning. "We planned on offering it to you, so you could give it to that little human you're infatuated with and gift her with eternity."

Really? "And what would you demand of me?"

Riel spun the Black Thorn around his fingers, and Nasya watched him with big, scared eyes. She didn't dare to move. "Kill Levi," he said.

What?

"And make sure his soul doesn't come back," Jed added.

That would mean the end of balance. Forever. There would be no way of restoring the creed or peace in the world. Imha's chaos would spread and infect everything, everyone. No, that couldn't happen.

I still had one advantage here. I was trapped within a shield, but the cup was in my hands. They would have to bury that Black Thorn deep in my chest to pry it from my fingers.

I needed a plan.

I squared my shoulders. "I'll do it."

Amiel tilted his head with suspicion. "If it was thirty years ago, I would have dropped the shield at once and let you go, no questions asked. But you've changed. You're not the same Mitrus we knew. How can you guarantee us you'll do it?"

So he was the one holding the shield up. I kept on my poker face. "I hate the guy. Levi thinks he's all that just because he's the center of the creed. He carries himself as if we have to kiss the ground he walks on. Just because he died with me and we were collaborating to recover our powers, doesn't mean we're allies now. I endured him because I had to."

The four of them exchanged wary looks. I didn't think they were buying it.

"That's not enough," Keon said. "We need proof or a physical guarantee."

I knew what he was asking. To leave the Cup of Life with them until after I had killed Levi. They were backing me into a corner, and I had to break free before it was too late.

My eyes met Nasya's. She was vulnerable here, and I couldn't guarantee her safety. I hoped she sensed my intentions and was ready for it. She gave me the slightest nod.

"You cowards," she said, drawing the Death Lords' attention to her.

I cast a black bolt and threw it at them. The bolt hit Amiel's back and Jed's side, causing them to fall over Riel and Nasya. She yelped, scooting away.

I extended my hand forward, half-expecting it to bump the invisible wall again, but it didn't. The wall had fallen with Amiel. I clutched the Cup of Life tighter and raced across the bridge, firing bolts at Riel, who chased after Nasya, and Keon, who turned to me with a death stare.

He produced a ball of energy, but I had already thrown mine. It exploded on his shoulder, and he staggered back. I cast a shield between us and kept on running, with one thought on my mind: reach the edge of the shield.

Nasya shot up and ran, but she didn't get too far as Riel cast chains around her legs. She fell on the grass again.

Something tugged inside me, something similar to sympathy. I slowed down and, using magic, undid the chains around her and tied them around Riel. He broke the chains in no time and turned to me, allowing Nasya to run away into the darkness of the island.

Keon broke the shield. Jed stood up, grunting from my shot, and Riel actually growled, charging me.

Fuck.

The power in me demanded I turn and fight like the real god I was, but that would be foolish. I had to stun them again, throw them off and keep running until I was on the dock. If I tried to fight, I would spill the elixir, or lose the cup to them —options I didn't want to consider.

I hurried along the path, sensing the three of them coming after me, hearing their groans and heavy footsteps.

I was already on the sand when one of their bolts hit my leg and I tripped. My blood turned to ice as I focused on the cup, holding it up while I fell on my knees. A drop swished over the edge.

"Damn it," I cursed, scurrying to my feet. I tossed a bolt back, not really aiming, just hoping it hit one of them. Or all of them if I was lucky enough.

It wasn't my day. They dodged the bolt, slowing down a bit, and Jed lost his balance for a second. Then they were at it again.

Fuck.

I stepped onto the dock, and the swoosh of a bolt flying past my head made me stiffen. They were close, too close. I hurried my steps.

Something hot burned on my back. A bolt. I staggered

forward, focusing on the cup. Another bolt exploded on my shoulder. I fell forward, and the cup flew from my hand. I saw the golden cup clambering on the wooden boards, and the liquid splashing all over the deck, into the ocean. Panic gripped me. But the cup didn't hit the ground. It literally flew. I dragged myself to a half-sitting position. Riel used his powers to control the cup.

"No," I muttered. I cast the same spell and fought for the cup.

From the corner of my eye, I saw Keon producing a bolt to hit me, so I put up a shield. His bolt exploded on the shield, breaking it and shaking the dock. Another ball of energy came through the broken pieces and hit my shoulder—son of a bitch, it burned!—pushing it back. I lost my hold on the cup, and Riel grasped it.

My heart stopped. *No.*

"It's ours now," he said, rather proudly.

Grunting, I stood. "Hand it to me. That's an order."

They laughed as Amiel appeared from the end of the path, limping.

"See, Amiel," Keon said. "Mitrus ordered us to hand the Cup of Life to him."

Without a word, Amiel conjured an energy ball and flung it at me. With my hands free, I conjured my scepter and used it to put up a wall, but it was gone the moment the ball touched it. Then Riel cast a bolt, Jed fired another, and Keon threw a fourth one. I cast shield after shield, waiting for an opening to toss one of my bolts, but four against one wasn't fair, even if I was more powerful than they were.

With the scepter, the shields were stronger and held a little longer, for three or four bolts, allowing me to fire some of my own. However, I had four opponents and they didn't stop moving, making it hard for me to aim and hit.

I moved too, but forward because the only way to recover the Cup of Life would be getting to them.

The four of them cast one big ball of energy and sent it at me. I conjured a wall, but the bolt broke and it still kept coming, exploding on me. Air squeezed out of me and I flew back, hitting my back on the hard wood several feet away.

I groaned as pain spread through my back and my chest. I blinked, willing the dizziness away, but instead of the dark sky, their four faces hung over me.

Keon, Riel, and Jed held my arms and shoulders, and Amiel kicked my scepter away.

Amiel crouched over my legs, taking the Black Thorn from Riel, and turned his dark expression to me. "Not so tough now, huh? If you hadn't been so worried about leaving, you probably could have taken the four of us out before you lost the cup. You are powerful enough. But leaving was more important, right? So you could go to your human. Guess what? We've got the Cup of Life now." He whirled the Black Thorn in his hand. "And you're gonna do what we ask, or your human will never hear about the elixir of immortality." He lowered his hand, placing the tip of the Black Thorn over my heart. "And we'll tell Levi you've been plotting with Imha against him *again*."

I jerked, trying to get rid of Riel, Jed, and Keon, but Amiel pierced the tip of the Black Thorn into my skin.

A scorching pain spread from my chest, to my heart, my lungs, and my throat. I gasped as the burn took over me, burning like liquid fire. My vision blackened and my senses faded.

No! Desperation clutched at my heart.

"Kill Levi," Amiel said somewhere out of the darkness surrounding me. "Once you do, meet us in Machu Picchu at the underworld entrance hidden there. Come alone. We'll give you the Cup of Life, and then you'll be able to be with your human forever."

The pressure in my chest diminished, but the power of the Black Thorn was already in effect. My insides screamed, and my mind burned. I couldn't move, couldn't see, and couldn't hear.

An old friend found me—total blackness.

9

———

Groaning, I rolled on my bed and buried my face in the pillow, trying to avoid the bright sunlight. Sweet honey scent teased my senses.

I stiffened. Honey? Sunlight?

I sat up on the mattress, groaning once more when pain shot through my chest. What the hell? The blanket slipped from under my arms and, finding myself shirtless, I saw a small black dot over my heart and several lines spreading from it, as if someone had tattooed a small spiderweb on my chest.

I touched the web and remembered. The island, the test, the Cup of Life, the Death Lords, the Black Thorn. Oh fuck.

By the Everlast, I had failed. I had gone to the island, and I had passed the test. I had held the Cup of Life, just to lose it. That couldn't be true, because if it was true, it meant Nadine would die soon and that was unacceptable.

"It isn't as bad as it looks. Not anymore," Nasya said, entering the room with some sticks in her arms. "If they had pierced it any deeper though ..."

She had another transparent dress on. To avoid looking at her, I scanned the place. We were in a large room, with beige stone walls, high ceilings, and round columns. There were chaises, pillows, and rugs everywhere. A fire pit roared in the center of the room. That was my sunlight.

"Where are we?" I asked. My chest prickled, and I rubbed it. Damn thing.

Nasya threw the sticks on the fire. "My home. It's on the other side of the island." Then she turned and sashayed toward me.

She sat on the mattress and, uncomfortable with her nearness, I swung my legs to the other side, but groaned when a new pang burned my insides.

She rested her hand on my arm. "Take it easy, my Lord. You had a rough patch."

"I need to go. I still should be able to track them, to find the trace of their aura and follow it. I'll fi—"

"Lord Mitrus, you've been unconscious for three days."

I froze. "What?"

She nodded. "I thought you wouldn't make it, but finally yesterday you started healing."

Wouldn't make it? What the fuck? That little prick almost killed me? "I didn't know the Black Thorn could be used like that."

"I didn't either." She reached to the small table beside the mattress. "The Death Lords left this with you," she said, taking the Black Thorn from the table. Ignoring the pain, I jumped to my feet and put some distance between us. She looked hurt. "If I wanted you dead, I wouldn't have treated your wounds. In fact, I could have used this the moment the Death Lords left."

It made sense, but it was hard for me to come to terms with it. After all, she was holding a Black Thorn.

I sat on a chaise several feet from the mattress and raked my hands through my hair.

What would I do? I couldn't kill Levi. It would mean the end of the world, and I wanted a world, a better world, a safe world, where Nadine could live forever. But she couldn't live forever without the Cup of Life.

I couldn't go back to NYC and face them both, knowing I had to pick between them.

A new weight fell on my shoulders, and I sighed.

"I have something that will make you feel better," Nasya said, standing up.

Was she talking about her and her sensual body? No, thank you. I was already in too big of a mess. I had no mind or will for another. Surprising me, she walked away from me. She picked a silver bowl from a corner and brought it over. She knelt before me, handing me the bowl.

I closed my hands around it and felt what it was. "Water from the underworld lake."

"Yes," she said, retreating to the mattress. "It was a gift from Imha, like a compensation for making me a prisoner of this island." She gestured to the bowl. "You can watch over your human. Seeing her will probably make you feel better."

"She's not *my* human. She's a person, owner of herself." Though, with the Soul Oath, I was her owner actually. What a mess.

"You love her," Nasya said, a tint of jealousy in her tone.

I didn't answer, mostly because I didn't want to share my feelings with her. Instead, I focused on the water and called upon Nadine.

A black shadow covered the water, spinning in a whirl-wind, and revealing Nadine.

She was entering the gym where Keisha exercised. She wore black yoga pants and a pink bra top, similar to the ones she had on when I last saw her. Her hair was still loose, falling in a wave down her back, the way I liked it.

Keisha stopped whatever she was doing and smiled. "Finally. I thought you were going to stay in your bedroom until after we won the war."

"Three days of sulking was too much," Nadine said, pulling her hair up in a ponytail. "I'm back to myself now."

Wait, Nadine had been in her bedroom? For days? Because of what?

"She's beautiful, even though she looks sad," Nasya said.

She was beautiful, and she did look sad. And frustrated. And pissed off.

"Next time slap some sense into me and don't let me waste three days for nothing."

"Ha, I might enjoy that." Keisha went back to her exercises. "Hey, uh, Lady Izaera came back a few hours ago. She's talking to Zelen now about something related to forests and nymphs. I think she may have found another ally." She shrugged. "And Lady Ceris and Lord Levi are still out."

Nadine started on stretching exercises. "Searching for the other gods?"

"Yes." Keisha pressed her lips into a thin line. "They also hope to find Lord Mitrus." Nadine stilled. Keisha took a step toward her but stopped. "Tell me what happened, why you were so mad and depressed after he left that you closed your-self in your bedroom for three days." I sucked in a sharp breath. She did what? Because of me? "I don't mean to pry, but every girl needs a friend. You opened up to me before.

Know that I'm here for when you want to talk again. About anything."

Nadine resumed her movement. "Thanks, but I'm fine. A man who makes a girl cry doesn't deserve her tears."

"So he did make you cry?" Keisha asked. Nadine shot her a killer glance. "Sorry, sorry. Lady Ceris and Lord Levi will find him, you know. They will bring him home."

"I don't see why. He left. He chose to leave. Only the Fates know for what. We are better off without him." Sighing, she shook her head and whispered, "I'm better off without him."

My heart stopped. Not wanting to hear anymore of how I had hurt her, I broke the vision and put the bowl aside.

"I'm sorry, my Lord," Nasya said.

Yeah, I was sorry too.

Since Nasya had to cut my shirt to treat my wound, she gave me another one. It was old, like centuries old, but it was the only thing she had—and it probably belonged to her protector. I looked down at it—dirty white with frills on the sleeves. I made a mental note to change it as soon as an opportunity presented itself. I put it on, grabbed my jacket from the chaise, and stashed the damned Black Thorn in an inside pocket.

I turned to Nasya. "Thank you."

She bowed. "You're welcome, Lord Mitrus." She walked with me to the door of her home. "Where will you go now?"

At first, I didn't answer. Why should I? She was nothing to me, but I needed to vent. "I'm not sure. I think I'll try to find Amiel, Jed, Keon, and Riel. It's the only option I can see."

"But they are four, and you're one. Look at what they did to you the last time."

I didn't need to look. I could feel the damn web prickling under my skin, hurting, burning. "I'll be prepared this time." That was the plan, though I wasn't sure what I would do to be prepared exactly.

I thanked her once more.

She gave me a small smile. "Be careful."

Nodding, I walked away.

For days, I roamed the Earth, stopping by every relevant point—places the Death Lords and I used to meet to discuss plans and orders or just to hang out, their former hometowns when they had been humans, checkpoints to the underworld, and more. I found no trace of their auras. Nothing. It was as if they were gone from this world. Or after years of hiding from Imha, they actually got good at it.

In the end, I even stopped by Machu Picchu and spied the entrance to the underworld at the Intihuatana ritual stone. Of course, the Death Lords weren't here. They would have heard of Levi's death, they would have felt it, and they would come here only then.

There was no way around it. I had a hard choice to make: Levi and the fate of the entire world—the logical choice—or Nadine and my selfishness—my heart's choice.

Thank you for reading *Cup of Life*!

Reviews are very important for authors. If you liked my book, please consider leaving a review on amazon and/or on goodreads, please!

And you can read the first chapter of *Everlasting Circle* on the next page!

EVERLASTING CIRCLE

CHAPTER ONE

NADINE

THREE WEEKS, TWO DAYS, EIGHT HOURS, AND FORTY-SEVEN minutes.

That was how long Micah had been gone. But who was counting? Not me. Because I didn't care. Not anymore.

Or so I told myself.

Instead of obsessing about why he left with no explanation, I immersed myself in training with Keisha, in planning with Ceris, and in learning more about the creed with Victor —though he warned me that not even he remembered all the stories and legends. Meanwhile, Ceris had found four deities to work as scouts—Rihan, Tuzin, Nyria, and Letos, who would spy on Imha's and Omi's activities—and Izaera and Zelen spent several days at a time away, looking for more forest protectors, nymphs, or any kind of nature-related deities to join our group. Ceris called it an army, but we were only seven so far. Seven wasn't an army.

I tried to focus on each step I took, but it never worked. Instead, my mind always got away from me when I was running. It was hard to believe all that had happened in the last six months. I had found Victor, the guy I had been having visions of for ten months, and Micah, a guy I didn't see coming, but he rocked my world. Then, I found out they were actually gods—Micah was Mitrus, the god of death and the dead and the underworld, and Victor was Levi, the god of balance, life, and spirit. Even worse was to find out a good friend, Cheryl, was actually another goddess in disguise and that she had manipulated my life for almost a year. She had even manipulated my feelings for Victor, making me crazy about him, just to snatch him from me in the end. And there was so much more ... we found Morgan, a high priest, and Keisha, a freaking hero. We encountered Imha and Omi more times than I dared to admit, and they even captured and tortured me ... and killed my family. We were betrayed and hurt and broken apart one too many times. But we were still here, fighting against the darkness Imha and Omi had descended upon our world.

I had been running on the treadmill for seventy-three minutes when an idea popped in my head. Why hadn't I thought of it before? Ceris wanted an army. Maybe I could give her one.

I stopped the treadmill, and jumped off it.

"What is it?" Keisha asked, mildly out of breath from running on the treadmill beside mine. Her dark skin glistened with sweat, and her long black ponytail bounced side to side.

"Just ... need to see something." I grabbed the towel from the treadmill and dabbed my damp face.

I walked into the living room, still finding it odd not

seeing Zelen seated on the floor, praying. The air here smelled faintly of lavender. Ceris had made it her mission to prevent the foul air outside from entering the apartment, so she kept scented candles lit all the time in all the rooms.

After I quickly washed my hands and face in the half-bath adjacent to the apartment's foyer, I went back to the living room. Where would Ceris have put it? I searched the TV stand, the shelves, under the coffee table. I moved on to the dining room, our usual meeting room, and searched the buffet cabinet and inside the many books Ceris had brought from all over the world that were not crowding the dining room. The walls were lined with books—sans-shelves—sorted in piles as high as my chest. Nothing in here either.

I considered the kitchen, but Ceris wouldn't have hidden it in the kitchen. Where else, then? I wouldn't search her bedroom.

"What are you looking for?" Ceris asked from behind me.

I turned to her. As usual, her sight made me self-conscious. She was a goddess—the goddess of love, family, home, and beauty—and she was stunning. Her long white hair fell down her back like a cascade of silver, her clear blue eyes shone with power, her skin was smooth, unblemished, and her figure ... well, she was a goddess.

"The map," I answered.

She extended her hand between us and the rolled map appeared in her outstretched palm. "Here." I took it from her, sat on the couch, and unrolled the yellowed map with torn edges on the coffee table. Ceris sat beside me. "What are you looking for?"

The bright symbols came to life on the paper, sprouting all around the map. They didn't rush around like the first time I had seen them. This time, most of them were still in their places, some shining brighter than the others.

"What are the other gods' symbols?" I asked.

"You're going to try to find them?" Victor asked, entering the living room.

I looked up and nodded. His beauty didn't have the same effect on me as it had when we first met, but I couldn't deny he was handsome. Gorgeous even. With honey-colored hair, sea-green eyes, fair skin, a chiseled face, and a tall, strong figure, who wouldn't think he was gorgeous? Moreover, he was a god. His power was as tangible and suffocating as Ceris's.

"That's a good idea," Ceris said.

She produced a book with a worn leather cover out of thin air. *The Gods and Goddess of the Everlasting Circle.* Ugh, I knew this book. I had skimmed through it less than two months ago. It belonged to Morgan, a high priest. He was now in the underworld and I had put him there.

The hurt snaked its way into my chest. It hit fast and hard, and it became difficult to breathe. Just like every night when I woke up from the same nightmare.

"Nadine?" Victor asked. He sat on the arm of the sofa beside Ceris.

I shook that feeling aside—just aside, because it never left me—took the book from Ceris, and opened to the chapters about the other gods and goddesses—Sol, god of the sun and day; Lua, goddess of the moon and night; Ronen, goddess of entertainment and arts; and Maho, god of magic—and tried to memorize their symbols. All of the major gods and goddess symbols were encased in a circle, so it was easy to distinguish from the rest. I couldn't find Sol's symbol, Lua's and Ronen's kept flashing all over the map, but Maho's was strong and on a little island in Thailand.

I pressed the tip of my index finger on the map. "This is Maho. He must be there."

"The Phi Phi Islands, of course," Victor said, leaning over the map. "We should go there."

"Now?" Ceris asked. "But Izaera and Zelen aren't here. It would be only the four of us, and ..." She paused, looking at me.

"And I count for almost nothing?" I replied, being careful not to show how much her comments hurt sometimes. "I know, but that's what you got."

"We can go, scout the place," Victor said, trying to appease Ceris. "If we see it's clear, we proceed. If there are demons or trouble, we fall back and summon Izaera and Zelen."

I sighed. If Micah were here, we would have three full gods instead of two. But he wasn't, and I had to accept that. Why was it so hard, damn it?

Ceris sighed. "All right. Let's go."

I stood and inhaled deeply. One more step toward the end.

The end. Soon, it would be the end of the war. We would win—I had to believe that—and break thirty years of darkness, or we would lose, leaving Imha and Omi to reign over the world, spreading chaos and terror.

Regardless of the outcome, my end would come. That was, of course, if Micah returned to finish our deal.

ABOUT THE AUTHOR

While USA Today Bestselling Author Juliana Haygert dreams of being Wonder Woman, Buffy, or a blood elf shadow priest, she settles for the less exciting—but equally gratifying—life as a wife, a mother, and an author. Thousands of miles away from her former home in Brazil, she now resides in North Carolina and spends her days writing about kick-ass heroines and the heroes who drive them crazy.

Subscribe to her mailing list to receive emails of announcement, events, and other fun stuff related to her writing and her books: www.bit.ly/JuHNL

For more information:
www.julianahaygert.com

ALSO BY JULIANA HAYGERT:

Free

Into the Darkest Fire

Tested

Secret Santa

The Everlast Series

Destiny Gift (Book 1)

Soul Oath (Book 2)

Cup of Life (Book 3)

The Everlasting Circle (Book 4)

Willow Harbor Series

Hunter's Revenge (Book 3)

Siren's Song (Book 5)

The Breaking Series

Breaking Free (Book 1)

Breaking Away (Book 2)

Breaking Through (Book 3)

Standalones

Playing Pretend

Captured Love

Dazzle Me